BEAUTY AND THE BEAST

GIANFRANCESCO STRAPAROLA

Once upon a time there was a rich merchant who had three daughters. One winter there was a terrible storm at sea and the merchant lost all of his ships. The family had to sell their grand house and move to a tiny cottage. The older girls grumbled and complained about being poor. But the youngest, called Beauty because of her sweet face and gentle nature, made the best of it.

One day their father heard that one of the ships had survived the storm. As he left for town, he asked the girls what presents they would like him to bring back.

"A beautiful dress for me!" said the first daughter.

"A silver necklace!" said the second.

"What about you?" he asked Beauty. "There must be something you would like."

"A red rose for my hair," said Beauty with a smile.

The merchant had a miserable time in town sorting out his business, and he left no richer than when he'd arrived. On the way home snow began to fall, and the unlucky man soon realized he was lost. Suddenly, he found himself before a pair of locked, wrought-iron gates. Through the gates he could see a huge mansion with lights glowing warmly in the windows.

"If only I could shelter here," he said. At these words the gates swung open. The wind blew him toward the steps of the house and before he had time to knock, the door opened by itself. Inside was a table set with the most tempting food and drink.

He looked back through the swirling snow and saw that the gates had silently closed. As he stepped inside, the door creaked shut behind him.

He stood in the room, looking around nervously. One of the chairs pulled itself back from the table, as if inviting him to sit down. "Well, I'm obviously welcome here!" he thought. And he ate and drank as much as he could.

In front of the fire was a big sofa, covered with a fur rug. A corner of the rug turned back as if to say, "Do come and lie down." So that's what he did.

The next thing he knew it was morning. He sat at the table where breakfast was waiting for him. There was even a red rose in a silver vase on the table.

"A red rose!" he cried. "How lucky. Now Beauty will have her present after all." After eating his fill, he stood up and plucked the rose from its vase.

At once, a terrible roar filled the air. The door burst open and there stood the most horrifying sight. It was dressed in a man's clothes — but instead of hands there were hairy claws and its head was a mass of tangled fur.

"Steal my rose, would you?" it snarled, showing its awful fangs. "What kind of thanks is that for the welcome I've given you?"

The merchant nearly died of fright. "Please forgive me, sir. It was for my daughter, Beauty. But I'll put it back at once, of course."

"Too late!" growled the Beast. "You must take it with you now . . . and send me your daughter in exchange."

"No!" gasped Beauty's father. "No!"

"Then I shall eat you this minute," roared the Beast.

"Better for you to eat me than my lovely daughter," said the unhappy man.

"If you send her, I will not harm her," answered the Beast. "You have my word on it. Now choose."

The girl's father agreed to the dreadful bargain. The Beast gave him a magic ring, which, if twisted three times, would bring Beauty to the Beast's lonely mansion.

Beauty's father had a miserable journey home. And it was even worse when he told his daughters what had happened.

"Did he really say he would not hurt me, Father?" asked Beauty.

"He gave his word, my darling."

Beauty kissed them all goodbye and said, "Give me the ring." Then she put it on and twisted it three times.

Almost at once she found herself in the Beast's mansion. But he was not there to meet her and she did not see him for many days.

Because the house seemed so welcoming, Beauty was not afraid. But she began to feel so lonely that she wished the Beast would come and talk to her — however horrible he looked.

One day, as she wandered in the garden, the Beast stepped out from behind a tree. Beauty could not stop herself from screaming as she covered her eyes.

"Don't be afraid, Beauty," he murmured, trying to keep the growl out of his voice. "I've only come to wish you good day and ask if you are enjoying your stay at my house."

"Well," said Beauty, taking a deep breath, "I'd rather be at home. But I am well looked after, thank you."

"Good," said the Beast. "Would you mind if I walked with you for a while?"

The two of them wandered around the garden. After that day the Beast often came to talk to Beauty.

One night, Beauty saw him loping across the moonlit lawn. She realized with a shock that he was out hunting for his food. Glancing up, he saw her at the window. Covering his face with his great paws, he let out a roar of shame.

Although he was ugly, the Beast was very kind to Beauty. And because she was so lonely she began to look forward to seeing him.

One evening while Beauty was reading by the fire, the Beast said hopefully, "Marry me, Beauty."

Beauty felt sorry for him. "I do like you very much, Beast," she said, "but I don't love you." Though he often asked her again, she always refused as kindly as she could.

One day he found her weeping by the fountain in the garden. "Oh, Beast!" she moaned. "I'm sorry to cry when you've been so kind to me, but I'm homesick. I miss my father so much."

To her joy, Beast said, "You may go home for seven days if you promise to come back." Beauty promised at once and twisted the ring on her finger.

What happiness there was when Beauty appeared in the little kitchen in the middle of supper. They had a wonderful time together. At the end of the week there was no sign or word from the Beast.

"Perhaps he's forgotten," thought Beauty. "I'll stay just a little longer."

Another week passed and there was still no word. The family breathed a sigh of relief.

Then one night as Beauty was brushing her hair in front of the mirror, her reflection suddenly faded. There instead was the Beast. He was lying by the moonlit fountain almost hidden by fallen leaves.

"Oh, Beast!" cried Beauty, tears springing to her eyes. "Please don't be dead. I'll come back."

She twisted the ring three times and found herself by his side in the garden.

"Beast, oh, Beast," she wept, lifting his huge head onto her lap. "I didn't mean to kill you. I *do* love you." She tried to brush the leaves from his face, but her eyes were so full of tears that she could not see.

Suddenly, he spoke. "Look at me, Beauty. Wipe away your tears and see what you have done."

Beauty looked down and saw that she was stroking a head of golden hair. Beast had vanished and in his place was the most handsome of men.

"Who are you?" she gasped.

"I am a prince," he said. "A witch cast a spell on me to change me into a beast. Only true love could free me. Ah, Beauty, I'm so glad you came back. Now will you marry me?"

"Of course, my prince, I will." And the two of them lived happily ever after.

Alan Baker

The tale of **Beauty and the Beast** was first introduced into European literature by the Italian author Gianfrancesco Straparola. In his book, *Piacevoli notti* (*The Nights of Straparola*), written between 1550 and 1553, Straparola collected 75 short prose tales drawn from many sources. His version of the magical tale of Beauty and her Beast captured the imagination of many other authors; a French translation by Mademoiselle de Villeneuve gave the tale an even wider audience. In 1946 Jean Cocteau directed a film based on the tale.